One Riddle, One Answer

by LAUREN THOMPSON

Illustrated by LINDA S. WINGERTER

SCHOLASTIC INC.

New York Toronto London Auckland
Sydney New Delhi Hong Kong

For Robert, my "one" and only
L.T.

For Mum and Karl, who brought me here
L. S. W.

Scholastic is constantly working to lessen the environmental impact of our manufacturing processes.
To view our industry-leading paper procurement policy, visit www.scholastic.com/paperpolicy.

This book was illustrated using acrylics on Bristol board.
The text type was set in Eva Antiqua Heavy.
Book design by Kristina Albertson.

ISBN-13: 978-0-590-31337-7
ISBN-10: 0-590-31337-1

3 4 5 6 7 8 9 10   40   21 20 19 18 17 16 15

Long ago in Persia, there lived a powerful sultan. He had many sons, but only one daughter, named Aziza, and he wished for her a wise and happy life. The finest tutors in the land were brought to the palace, and Aziza learned all there was to know. But her favorite subject was numbers. And her favorite game was riddles.

The time came for Aziza to marry. The sultan began to seek a suitable husband for her.

"Who in the land is most worthy of her hand?" the sultan asked his advisors.

"My eldest son is very handsome, your honor," said one advisor.

"My youngest son is very clever," said another.

It seemed that all of the sultan's advisors had only their own sons to recommend. The sultan was angry.

"You have advised enough!" cried the sultan, and he sent his advisors away.

Then Aziza went to the sultan.

"Father," she said, "perhaps there is a better way to choose whom I should marry."

The sultan knew his daughter was wise and good, and above all he wished her to be happy. "Tell me your plan," he said.

"Let me pose a riddle," said Aziza. "The riddle has but one true answer. Whoever can answer the riddle will be the one I would be happiest to marry."

"A riddle?" asked the sultan.

"Yes," said Aziza. "Here it is."

PLACED ABOVE, IT MAKES GREATER THINGS SMALL.

PLACED BESIDE, IT MAKES SMALL THINGS GREATER.

IN MATTERS THAT COUNT, IT ALWAYS COMES FIRST.

WHERE OTHERS INCREASE, IT KEEPS ALL THINGS THE SAME.

WHAT IS IT?

The sultan thought for a moment, and then he sighed. "This riddle is too difficult even for me. In all the land, there is no man who will solve this riddle."

"Perhaps there will be one," Aziza said. "And one is all that is needed."

So the sultan agreed to Aziza's plan.

The next day, Aziza set out with a caravan in search
of the one who could solve the riddle. In every city,
town, and village, a messenger spread the news of the
sultan's daughter's riddle.

"One riddle, one answer! Let any number try!" cried
the messenger. "Only one will win the hand of the
sultan's daughter!"

Every place they stopped, men young and old tried to
solve the riddle. But none had the answer.

In one village, a scholar came before Aziza to announce his answer. He was an astronomer, who studied the movements of the sun, moon, and stars.

"I have observed that the answer is the sun," he said with much confidence. "For the riddle speaks of shadows. When the sun is high above us, even the greatest man seems small, as he has only a small shadow. Thus, the answer is the sun."

"A learned answer indeed," said Aziza. "But that is not the right answer to the riddle."

In another town, a soldier came before Aziza with his answer.

"A sword!" he cried, displaying his gleaming saber. "The answer must be a sword. For the riddle speaks of war. And in war, even the smallest man is great in strength with a sword by his side."

"You have given a strong answer," said Aziza. "But that is not the right answer to the riddle."

In another city, a merchant came before Aziza.
"Honored lady," he said sweetly, "your clever riddle
has been solved. The riddle speaks of the ways of the
world, and the answer, therefore, is money. For as
everyone knows, in all matters that count, money
always comes first." He smiled at Aziza, sure that he
had won her hand.

"Your answer is more clever than my riddle," said
Aziza wearily. "But your clever answer is wrong."
"May I try another riddle?" asked the merchant.
"No," Aziza said. "One riddle, one answer."

Aziza felt discouraged. Perhaps her father was right.
Perhaps no one in the land would know the answer
to the riddle. She ordered the caravan to
return to her father's palace.

Just as the caravan was about to depart, a young man came forward. He was a farmer named Ahmed, and he too loved numbers.

"Will you hear one more answer?" Ahmed asked.

"Just one more," Aziza said, sighing.

"The riddle speaks of numbers," he said, "and the answer is the number one. For in a fraction, the number one placed above a large number makes a small number. One hundred is large, but one hundredth is small."

"Yes, it is," said Aziza. "Go on."

"And when the number one is placed beside another number," he said, "the number increases. One placed beside nine makes nineteen."

"Or ninety-one," said Aziza. She smiled.

"Or ninety-one," said Ahmed. He smiled back.

"And in counting," Ahmed went on, "the number one always comes first. That is as simple as one, two, three." "Yes!" said Aziza, laughing.

Ahmed said, "And in multiplication, the number one keeps the value of another number, while other numbers increase the value. One times ten is ten, but two times ten is twenty, and three times ten is thirty. And this is why," said Ahmed, "the answer to your riddle is the number one."

"That is a wonderful answer," said Aziza. "And it is right! With this answer, you have won my hand."

"With this riddle, you have won my heart," said Ahmed.

Aziza and Ahmed returned to the sultan's palace.
Before long, they were married.

The sultan made Ahmed his chief advisor
in matters of farming.
And he made Aziza his chief advisor in
matters of numbers.

HOW DID AHMED SOLVE AZIZA'S RIDDLE?

Aziza's riddle is made up of four parts, and to be right, an answer must work for all four parts of the riddle. Here again is Aziza's riddle:

PLACED ABOVE, IT MAKES GREATER THINGS SMALL.
PLACED BESIDE, IT MAKES SMALL THINGS GREATER.
IN MATTERS THAT COUNT, IT ALWAYS COMES FIRST.
WHERE OTHERS INCREASE, IT KEEPS ALL THINGS THE SAME.
WHAT IS IT?

The first suitors' answers were not right because they were true for only part of the riddle. The astronomer's answer, *the sun*, was right for the first part of the riddle, but not for all of the other parts. The soldier's answer, a *sword*, was right only for the second part of the riddle. And the merchant's answer, *money*, was right for only the third part of the riddle. But Ahmed's answer, *the number one*, was right for all four parts of the riddle. How?

PLACED ABOVE, IT MAKES GREATER THINGS SMALL.

First, Ahmed knew that in a fraction, if the number 1 is placed above a larger number, the resulting fraction is smaller than the original number. (Try it! 1 placed above 100 becomes 1/100; 1 placed above 1000 becomes 1/1000; and so forth.) In fact, the larger the number, the smaller the resulting fraction will be.

$$\frac{1}{100}$$

$$\frac{1}{1000}$$

PLACED BESIDE, IT MAKES SMALL THINGS GREATER.

Second, Ahmed saw that when the number 1 is placed beside a small number, that number becomes greater. So, 1 placed beside 9 becomes 19, which is larger than 9.

As Aziza pointed out, this rule also works when 1 is placed on the other side of the number. In this case, 9 becomes 91. (Try another example: 1 placed on either side of 27 becomes — what number? Is that number larger?)

19

91

IN MATTERS THAT COUNT, IT ALWAYS COMES FIRST.

Third, Ahmed recognized that "in matters that count," that is, in *counting*, the number 1 always comes first. We always start counting with 1. (Did you notice that other numbers would work for the first two parts of the riddle, but that only the number 1 works for this part? Ahmed noticed!)

$$1 \quad 2 \quad 3$$

WHERE OTHERS INCREASE, IT KEEPS ALL THINGS THE SAME.

Fourth, Ahmed saw that when multiplying, any number multiplied by 1 will stay the same: 1 times 10 is still 10; 1 times 999 is still 999. But multiplying by any other number will give an entirely different number: 2 times 10 is 20; 3 times 10 is 30; 4 times 999 is 3,996. So in this way, "Where others increase, *the number one* keeps all things the same." In this part of the riddle too, only one number could be the right answer, and that number is the number 1 — the *one* answer that Aziza was waiting for.

$$1 \times 10 = 10 \qquad 1 \times 999 = 999$$

As a farmer, Ahmed would have used mathematics every day, when he calculated the amount of pasture he would need for his sheep, the yield of grain he could expect from a field of barley, or how much to charge at the market. It was in Persia that many mathematical concepts were first developed, including algebra, trigonometry, and logarithms. Eight hundred years ago, the Persian system for writing numbers, which originally came from India, became popular in Europe, where the awkward Roman numeral system had been in use. Today, "Arabic numerals" are used around the world.